I0730431

To Peyton, Preston, and Madison.
Our hope for you is that you will discover the truth about
who you are, the beauty inside of you, and your purpose in life.
As you discover those things, our hope is that you will help others
realize their beauty, purpose, and identity as well.
We love each of you so very much!
Mom and Dad

To my grandmothers for their introducing me
to their love of gardens.
Carter

Garden Tales:
A Seed's Story

M any years ago, a seed named Sally was planted in the dirt. The gardener who planted her made sure to plant her at the right time of year, in the right environment, and with the nutrients he knew she needed to grow big and beautiful.

The gardener kept a **faithful** eye on her,

minute by **minute,**

and **day** by **day.**

He made sure Sally
got the right amount of sunshine,
water, and attention she needed to
grow and thrive!

As the days went by, Sally began to wonder **who** she was
and **what** she was made for.

Since she grew up in dirt,
looked like dirt, and was surrounded by dirt,
she believed she was dirt!

One day, Sally's friend, Max the mole, was walking by. She said to him, "Max, I've been trying to discover who I am. I think I have figured it out, but I would like your opinion."

She continued, "I was planted in this dirt. There is dirt all around me. I **must** be a piece of dirt. Do you think so, too?"

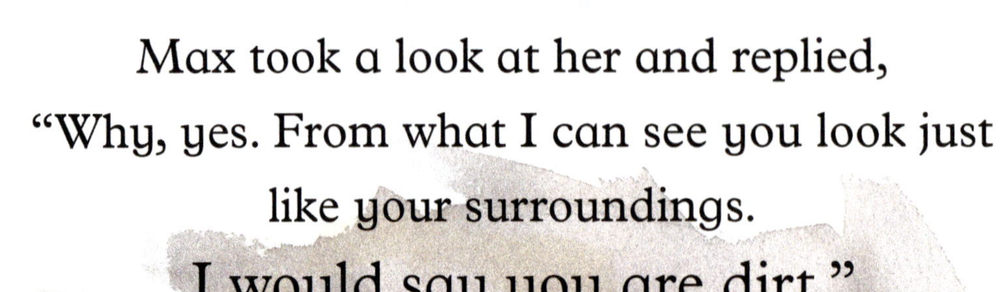

Max took a look at her and replied,
"Why, yes. From what I can see you look just
like your surroundings.
I would say you are dirt."

Max continued on his way.

After their conversation, Sally couldn't help but feel a little
sad that she wasn't a mole, a slug, or even an ant!
They seemed to have all the fun. They were able to crawl around,
and go wherever they wanted to go.

Sally was stuck.

With nowhere to go and nothing
to do, she started to feel like she had
no purpose at all.

Much time passed by.

One warm spring day,
the gardener approached Sally
and commented on what a
beautiful flower she was.
He looked at her,
and began to describe the
amazing design and
color he saw.
She was **puzzled** by
his words, and her
face showed it.

"Excuse me?" Sally said to the gardener, "I'm not
sure what you're talking about.
I grew up in the dirt and I'm surrounded
by dirt. I am just a piece of dirt.
Even Max the Mole agrees!

Can't you see?"

The gardener **kindly** looked back at her with the most **loving**, **compassionate** eyes she had **ever** seen. He quietly took out his camera, snapped a picture, and showed it to her.

Sally was **shocked** to discover the flower in the picture was her!

She was finally shown the truth about who she was.

The beauty she saw took her breath away.

It was hard for Sally to believe she was a flower
and not dirt, but as the days went by, she began to accept
that she was a **beautiful flower**.

Whenever she would begin to doubt the truth, she would use her
picture as a reminder of who the gardener said she was.

Sally was happy to have the gardener nearby as she discovered who she was, and what she was made for. He was a very patient, kind, and compassionate gardener.

He always took the time to speak with her about what was on her mind.

During one of their many talks, the gardener explained to Sally that it is a very special time when a flower blooms. They are created for that very purpose! The gardener shared with Sally that she brought him much **joy** and **pleasure**.

One day, Sally took a look around at the other flowers in the garden. She wondered if they believed **they** were dirt,

just as she had thought about herself.

She asked the gardener about this. He responded,

"Well, why don't you ask them?"

So Sally waved at the flower next to her. Her name was Trudy.
She began to tell Trudy how much she liked her color and design.
Before Sally could go into detail, Trudy stopped her and said,
"Excuse me, I grew up in the dirt and I'm surrounded by dirt.
I am just a piece of dirt. Can't you see?"

Sally responded by calling the gardener over so he could take a picture of Trudy. At that moment, Trudy was shown the **truth** about who she was.

As Sally watched her friend go through the same process she had gone through, she smiled to herself. **She had been given a wonderful gift.**

The gardener had changed Sally's life in a powerful way
by showing her the **truth** of who she was
and what she was made for.
Together, Sally and the gardener would help the flowers around her
realize their **beauty** and **purpose** as well.

As more flowers discovered the truth about themselves and what they were made for, the garden grew to be a much more **joyful** place to live. Deep in their hearts, the flowers knew they brought the gardener much pleasure.

He had changed their lives *forever*.

ISBN 13: 978-1-64590-007-8

Published by Kingdom Winds Publishing.

6 Charleston Oak Lane, Greenville, SC 29615

www.kingdomwinds.com

publishing@kingdomwinds.com

Printed in the United States of America.

The views expressed in this book are not necessarily those of the publisher.